Sammy Shark's Stomach Ache

Jennifer Storelli

MOOREFIELD HOUSE PUBLISHING

Jennifer Storelli/Moorefield House Publishing

7948 N. Neva Ave.

Niles, IL 60714

www.moorefieldhousepublishing.com

Publisher's Note: This is a work of fiction. Names, characters, places, and incidents are a product of the author's imagination. Locales and public names are sometimes used for atmospheric purposes. Any resemblance to actual people, living or dead, or to businesses, companies, events, institutions, or locales is completely coincidental.

Book design © 2017, BookDesignTemplates.com

Ordering Information: Special discounts are available on quantity purchases by corporations, associations, and others. For details, contact the publisher at the address above.

Niles / Jennifer Storelli — First Edition

ISBN 978-1-9470140-6-0

Printed in the United States of America

Sammy Shark's Stomach Ache

Jennifer Storelli

Something was wrong with Sammy Shark.

He tried to eat his tuna fish, but that hurt his teeth. He tried to eat some nice, soft seaweed, but his stomach groaned, "No!"

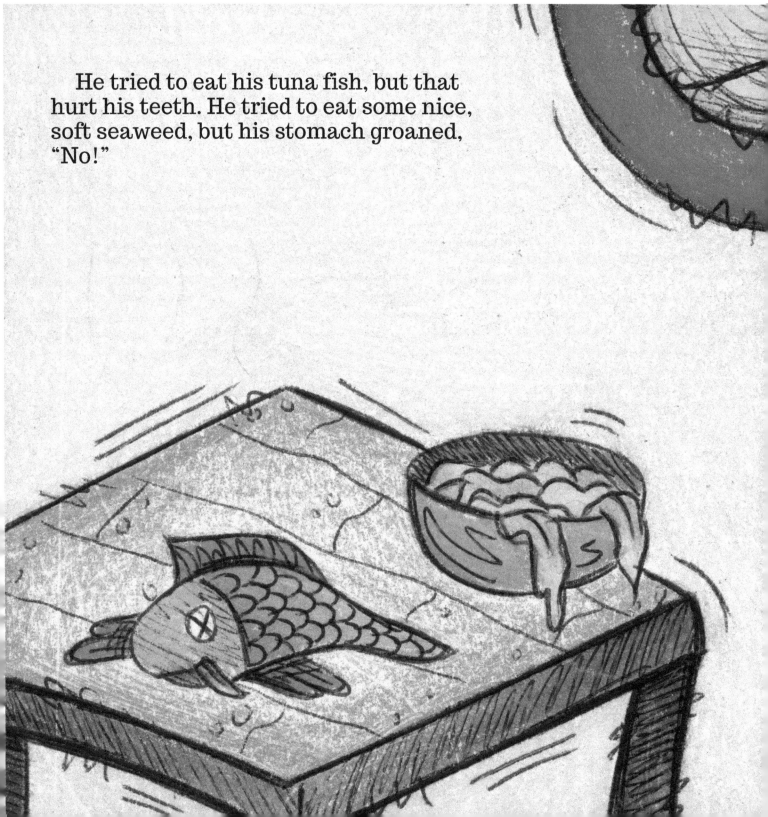

His stomach hurt. His teeth hurt. He couldn't even swim fast without feeling dizzy. Sammy knew something was wrong.

Sammy asked his neighbor Stacy Starfish what to do. She rubbed his tummy, but that didn't make him feel better.

Sammy asked his friend Stanley Shrimp to help too. Stanley brought a toothbrush and brushed Sammy's teeth, but that didn't help either.

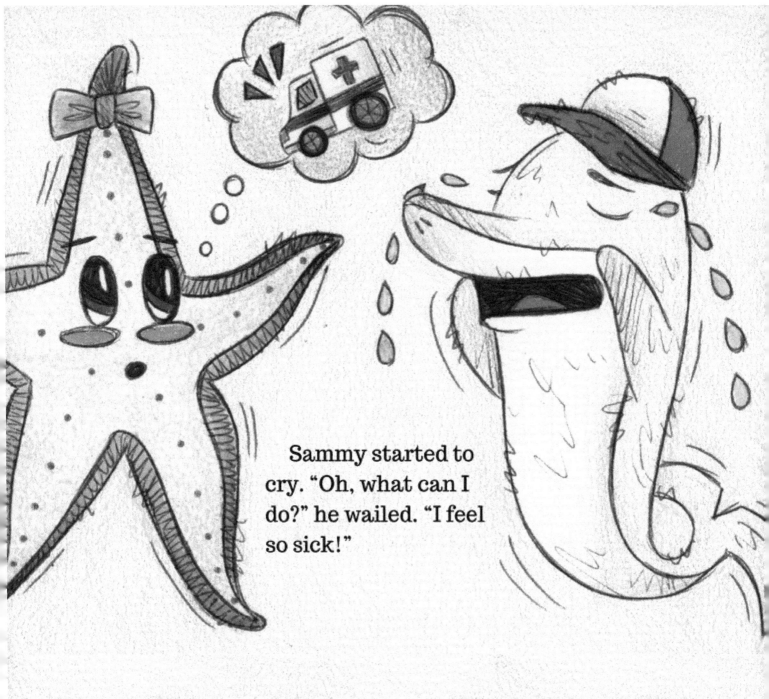

Sammy started to cry. "Oh, what can I do?" he wailed. "I feel so sick!"

Sammy's friends told him to go see the nurse shark. Sammy was afraid to go, so Stacy and Stanley went along to help Sammy feel better

At the nurse shark's office, Nurse Natalie poked and prodded Sammy's tummy and carefully checked all of his teeth. Some of his teeth were chipped, and there were strange bulges in his tummy. Nurse Natalie knew something was wrong.

"What have you been eating, Sammy?" Nurse Natalie asked.

"I don't really remember," he answered. "Some plankton, a lobster, some squid with a side of mollusk ..."

"Anything unusual?" Nurse Natalie questioned.

"Now that you mention it, last night I was exploring, and I found this pile of shiny food," Sammy explained. "It was different, though. It wasn't moving like my usual food does. This food came in different shapes and sizes, and all of it was hard."

Nurse Natalie thought for a moment and decided to take an X-ray of Sammy's stomach. The X-ray showed that there were many strange things in Sammy's stomach. Nurse Natalie found a small chain, a tin can, and even a license plate. "Sammy, these things are not really food," she explained.

Stanley laughed. "Sammy, how could you eat something that's not food?" he teased.

"It's not his fault," Nurse Natalie said. "Sharks are naturally attracted to shiny objects in the water."

"If it's not food, then what is it?" Sammy asked.

"It's garbage from humans," Nurse Natalie said.

"Humans?!?!" Sammy, Stacy, and Stanley exclaimed.

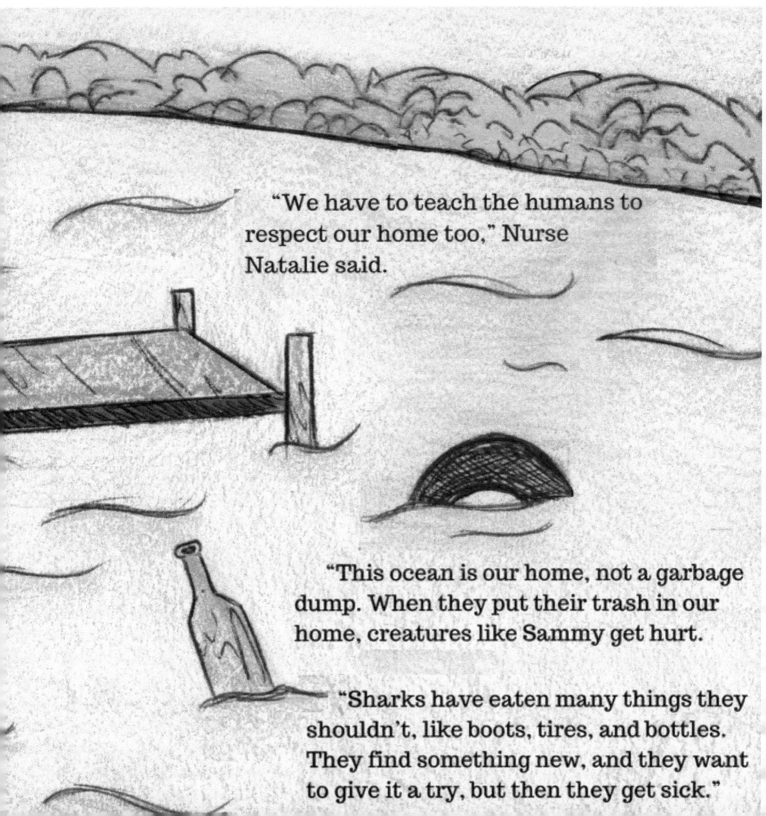

"We have to teach the humans to respect our home too," Nurse Natalie said.

"This ocean is our home, not a garbage dump. When they put their trash in our home, creatures like Sammy get hurt.

"Sharks have eaten many things they shouldn't, like boots, tires, and bottles. They find something new, and they want to give it a try, but then they get sick."

"Maybe we can work together with the humans to protect the whole world," Stacy added. "It's everyone's home, so we should all share the load and keep it clean so that it's a safe place for everyone."

Now that Sammy knows what garbage is, he is more careful about what he eats. He also teaches other sea creatures about garbage so that they don't eat it either.

Humans can also help Sammy and his friends by being careful with their garbage and recycling whenever they can. If we work together, we can all protect our earthly home.

About the Author:

Jennifer Storelli lives in Chicago with her husband. She has loved writing short stories since she was 8 and is happy to be living her dream as a children's book author. She also has a degree in journalism from Northwestern University and works as a magazine editor.

About the Illustrator:

Sarah Butkovic is a college freshman living in Chicago. She loved to draw with sidewalk chalk as a child. As she grew older, she began to unearth her passion for art. Her high school art teacher and parents continued to encourage, critique, and introduce Sarah to different methods and media.